This igloo book belongs to:

..............................................

**igloobooks**

Published in 2015
by Igloo Books Ltd
Cottage Farm
Sywell
NN6 0BJ
www.igloobooks.com

HUN001 0215
2 4 6 8 10 9 7 5 3 1
ISBN 9781-78440-538-0

Illustrated by Kate Leake

Printed and manufactured in China

# My MONSTER SMELLS GROSS!

igloobooks

One day I found a **monster**,
hiding inside the laundry box.
He was curled up asleep,
in a pile of my smelly socks.

He had **spiky, red** hair,
big horns and **furry** skin.
When he woke up, he smiled at me
with a **big, toothy grin.**

My monster likes revolting **stuff**,
like **furry** moths and slugs.
He also loves to **suck** the goo
from different sorts of bugs!

The **grimy, gross, disgusting**
dish my monster likes the most,
is sickeningly **squiggly,** wriggly **maggots**
spread on mouldy toast!

My **monster** likes to look his best,
everywhere he goes.
He bathes in **slimy swamps** and trims
the **green claws** on his toes.

He smoothes his hair with **fish oil** and
cleans his teeth with **mouldy** goo.
Under his arms he rubs old cheese
and that smells stinky, too!

In my tree house my monster plays
all sorts of **naughty** tricks.
He **picks** big lumps of **earwax**,
then licks his lips and flicks!

He loves to make **big, sloppy** cakes
and horrid cupcakes, too.
He covers them in **mud** and **mould**
and sometimes soft bird poo!

At my birthday party,
he put a yucky outfit on.
His waistcoat was made with snail shells
stuck together with **chewing** gum.

His shorts were covered with **stringy** slime
and **crusty** old cowpats.
On his hat were pink mouse tails
and flapping vampire **bats!**

Sometimes he gets greasy spots.
They're squishy and they're green.
When he's got a big one,
you'll know where he's been.

He loves to **squeeze** and **squash** it
and **squish** it, 'til it spurts.
He just loves to see how far
he can make the green pus squirt!

My monster loves a game of pretend,
we play it all the time.
We imagine we are pirates,
sailing on a **sea of slime.**

Our ship's flag is made from his old **pants**
and we wear **grubby** pirate vests.
We fight **scary** sea monsters
and use maps to find **treasure** chests.

He picked a fresh **bogey**,
loaded his catapult and pulled it back.
The bogies flew through the sky
and hit the poor birds with a **thwack!**

When we go away on holiday,
my monster **never** behaves.
Last year he got me lost
in some **slimy**, **grimy** **caves**.

He **stomped** in lots of sandcastles
and I **always** got the blame.
A holiday without him
just **wouldn't** be the same.

I know that my monster is naughty
and **never** does what he's told,
that's why he loves to eat **smelly**
mud and **bird poo** and mould.

Even though he's imaginary and
really just pretend,
he'll always be my **super smelly**,
**very** best friend.

# "Goodbye,
## smell you soon!"